BIG IDEAS

... for you, your home, and your family

by Eugenia Santiesteban

Designed by Rick DeMonico

ISBN 0-439-69613-5

12 11 10 9 8 7 6 5 4 3 2 1   5 6 7 8 9/0

Printed in the U.S.A.
First printing, April 2005

SCHOLASTIC INC.

NEW YORK   TORONTO   LONDON   AUCKLAND   SYDNEY
MEXICO CITY   NEW DELHI   HONG KONG   BUENOS AIRES

Hi, my name is Maya Santos!

I'm always filled with tons of ideas that I love to share with my twin brother Miguel, my two best friends Chrissy and Maggie, and my family — my mom Rosa, my dad Santiago, and our grandmother, whom we call Abuela. Not to mention anyone else who will listen!

I'm Miguel Santos!

Maya's right, she always has her great ideas. Usually, when I hear her say *"eso es"* ("that's it!"), I know I should run the other way, but some of her brainstorms end up being a lot of fun. Okay, so maybe *most* of them.

We've collected the very best ones for you to do! The fun starts as soon as you turn the page!

And don't forget about Paco! He's our pet parrot!

If you're like me, you love looking at pretty things and feeling relaxed while you're at home. That's why I love my funky bedroom that Mamá and Papi let me decorate myself. It was really fun deciding what colors to use, picking my comfortable bed, and finding cool things to put on the walls!

Maggie and Chrissy helped me with the decorating. If it weren't for Maggie, I never would have learned about *feng shui* (I have Maggie's grandmother to thank for my bedroom layout). Chrissy helped me pick out the cool colors. Maybe your friends will help you out, too!

Topic To Discuss:

Feng shui: An ancient Chinese practice of decorating to bring inner peace and balance to life. It comes from the terms for wind and water, or yin and yang, both of which mean balance in Chinese culture!

DECORATING ACTIVITIES

☀ If you like bright, sunny colors that make you smile, then maybe you're a Color Enthusiast. Get your parents' permission to paint and cover your walls in fun, rainbow shades.

☀ Dreaming of the baseball diamond or soccer field? If you've got a hobby that you can't stop thinking about, maybe a theme-based room is a good idea. Horses, sports, or music — whatever it is, you can live surrounded by your passion!

☀ Is peace and quiet important to you? (Miguel's always saying he never gets enough with me around!) Maybe a Zen-inspired room is what you need. Get rid of the clutter, paint it white, and add some plants for a relaxing place for rest and meditation.

☀ If you're like Miguel and me, your house is filled with objects reminding you of your culture. You can celebrate your background, and display your heritage in your own bedroom, too. Be proud of where you come from!

MAKING A LAMPSHADE

The best part about decorating your room is making cool stuff for it. Maggie, Chrissy, and I found out how to decorate our own lampshade. It's easy, and all you need is a regular paper drum shade, a tape measure, pencil, some fabric, scissors, and glue.

1. Taking the paper drum shade (you can probably find this at any regular craft store, or ask permission to use one already in your home), make two measurements. The first will be the height of the shade, and the next will be the width around it.

2. Take the measurements, and measure out the length and width on a piece of fabric, marking the dimensions in pencil. Leave an extra half-inch to each side to give you some room for mistakes.

3. Next cut the fabric using the pencil marks as your guidelines.

4. Put glue on the back of the cut piece of fabric, and then attach it to the shade, making sure to keep the edges even — and presto! You've got something beautiful to decorate your room!

When I discovered that everyone has a talent they can show off, I thought, *Why not host a talent show?*

Papi can play the guitar, Abuela can dance, and Maya . . . well, she always has her great ideas! You can get every-one together in your neighborhood and hold tryouts, or just have it in your own living room. No matter the size, everyone should have their moment to shine!

Except maybe for Paco and his singing. . . .

TALENT SHOW ACTIVITIES

WHAT'S YOUR TALENT?

☀ Do you sing to yourself in the shower? Practice dance moves in front of the television? Then set up a song-and-dance routine!

☀ Dreaming of an Oscar® one day? Find a script from your favorite movie, play, or poem, and act out a scene or recite a monologue.

☀ Like to get everyone laughing? Are you the class clown? Put your pen to paper, and write a comedy routine — just make sure there aren't any rotten tomatoes in the audience!

☀ Not so interested in the stage? More of a sports fanatic? Strut your stuff with a soccer ball, or practice your juggling instead! Athletes are talented, too!

Kids, don'T forgeT To rehearse for The big day! Remember, pracTice makes perfecT! And if you're Like me, you were born for The STage. ¡HoLa! PreTTy Bird! HeLLo!

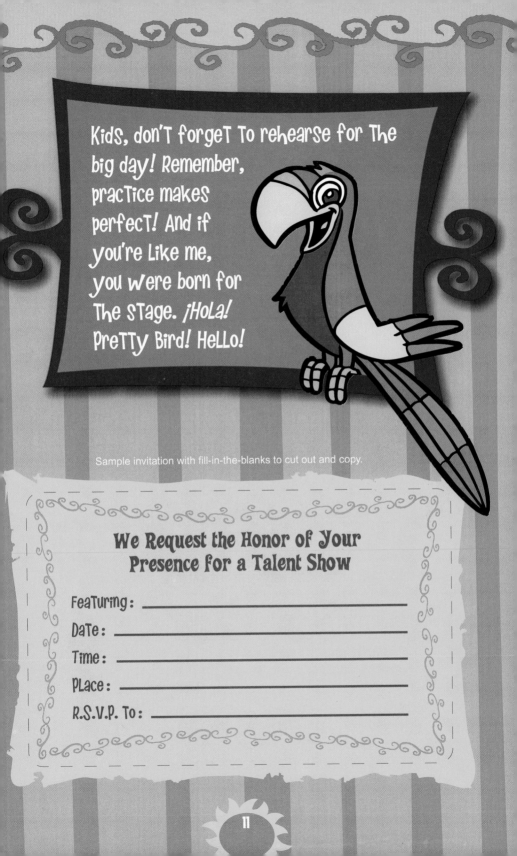

Sample invitation with fill-in-the-blanks to cut out and copy.

We Request the Honor of Your Presence for a Talent Show

FeaTuring: _____

DaTe: _____

Time: _____

PLace: _____

R.S.V.P. To: _____

COOKING A MEAL FOR FRIENDS & FAMILY

No one can cook Like AbueLa —

she makes the best guacamole for miles around! She used to have a restaurant, you know! And she still makes the best stuff — enchiladas, quesadillas, mmm. My mouth is watering just thinking about it. Luckily, she's a good teacher, too, and has let Maya and me in on some of her secret recipes!

Abuela loves it when people enjoy her food, so we've decided to share all these recipes with you. Make sure to ask for help in the kitchen, especially if you're using anything hot or sharp. Oh, and don't forget to clean up your mess — or your parents might never let you near the kitchen again!

QUESADILLA RECIPE

You will need tortillas (you can get either corn or flour), Monterey Jack cheese, and some chilies (or peppers if you like it spicy).

Place the tortilla on a plate. Cut four thin slices of cheese (each about 1 ounce), and place them on the center of the tortilla.

If you have a microwave, zap the plate on high for about 45 seconds, or until the cheese is melted. If not, ask an adult to turn on the stove, and cook for 1-2 minutes in a pan or griddle . . . or again, until the cheese is melted.

Add pepper or spicy sauce to your taste, fold your quesadilla in half, and enjoy!

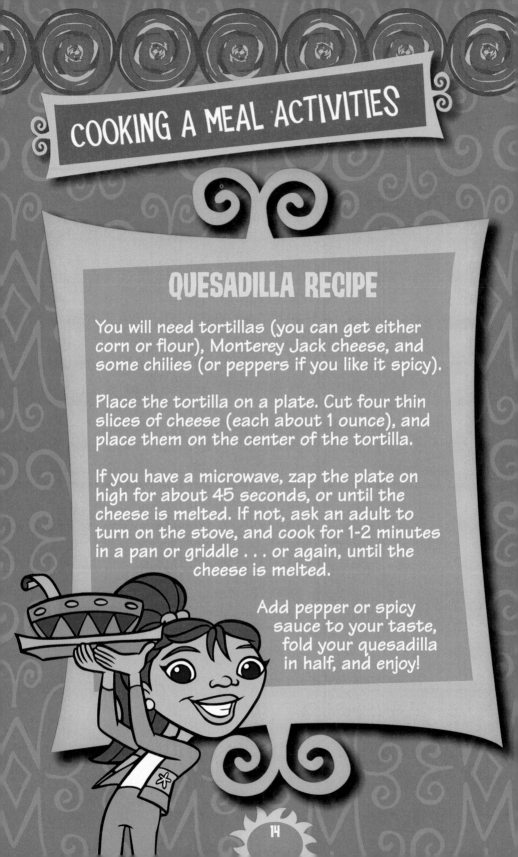

Q: When was the Tortilla invented?

A: The exact date that tortillas made from cornmeal were invented is not known. We do know that corn, or maize, was common in the diet of the Aztecs, and when Spanish conquistador Hernán Cortés arrived in Mexico in the early 16th-century he noted that the natives ate a corn flatbread called tlaxcallim. Later, the Europeans brought flour, giving rise to the flour-based versions, and today both are very popular in the United States and all over the world.

SAFETY IN THE KITCHEN

Remember to be extra safe whenever you're making anything in the kitchen, especially when using sharp knives or trying to reach high surfaces.

Always ask an adult to help whenever using the stove, oven, or the microwave.

Don't forget to make sure food has cooled off before eating — even though piping-hot dishes are hard to resist!

VACATION TIME

Okay, so maybe I'm used to everyone getting nervous when I have an idea. But I've got¡ a great one — a family vacation! I know Miguel, Mamá, Papi, Abuela, and Paco will have fun, too. The only hard part is deciding where to go — the beach, the mountains, camping — the possibilities are endless!

Not only will we have really important family bonding time, we also can learn about different places and cultures — even if the farthest we're going is only a town away!

Here are some ideas for trips you can take with your family. They don't have to be places far away. You can always organize a day at the beach, a nature hike, or a trip to the zoo . . . as long as it's something fun you can all do together!

VACATION TIME ACTIVITIES

PUTTING TOGETHER A SCRAPBOOK

You won't want to forget the special time you share together, so why not start a scrapbook to record all your wonderful memories?

* Take lots of pictures with your camera, or record your trip on video . . . or you can also sketch or paint a picture of your adventures instead.

* Collect keepsakes from the places you go. They'll help remind you of all the cool things you did.

* Get together all of the pictures and mementos, and organize them either by day, activity, or family member.

* Next, assemble them in a book, or get creative and make a huge collage. Your family will always remember the great time you all had!

DETERMINE YOUR VACATION STYLE

1. On my down time, I like to:
   A. Be really active — I can't ever sit still!
   B. Mostly read and get lots of rest.
   C. Get out and do things, but nothing that will make my heart rate go up too much!
   D. Try something I've never done before.

2. My favorite kind of climate is:
   A. I don't mind the weather, as long as I can be outside.
   B. Somewhere really sunny!
   C. Crisp and cool.
   D. Any kind that's different than where I live!

3. If I could pick anywhere in the world to go, it would be:
   A. Hiking near a mountain range.
   B. A beach in the Caribbean.
   C. A big city.
   D. Anyplace I've never heard of before.

If you picked mostly:

As: An active vacation sounds like it's the best for you. Hiking, skiing, and swimming will keep you from being bored.

Bs: You're a beach baby! Just make sure you wear some sunscreen.

Cs: You love the excitement and bustle of a big city.

Ds: You have a thirst for adventure and seeking out new things.

INTERNATIONAL DAY

I'm usually so busy thinking up great ideas that I don't even notice sometimes when they are right under my nose! Mamá and Papi are always teaching us about our heritage, and I love learning about it.

I think holding an International Day is really cool. You can cook authentic food, wear traditional clothes, and perform a dance or song from your ancestral country. And among my best friends — Maggie, Chrissy, and I — we have a lot of different cultures to share with the world.

INTERNATIONAL DAY ACTIVITIES

LANGUAGE 101

How to say, "Hello! How are you?"

In Spanish: ¡Hola! ¿Cómo está?
In French: Bonjour! Comment allez-vous?
In German: Hallo! Wie gehts?
In Portuguese: Hello. Como é você?
In Italian: Ciao. Come siete?

MATCH THE CONTINENT TO WHERE IT BELONGS ON THE MAP:

Africa, Antarctica, Asia, Australia, Europe, North America, South America

When I celebrated my Mexican heritage on International Day, I wore my hair in braids, and a serape, which is a colorful, embroidered wool wrap that once belonged to Abuela. I just searched in her trunk, but if you don't have someone you can borrow from, you can make your own costume. Research your country or culture, and use pictures to guide you. Even if it doesn't end up looking exactly like you wanted, they'll get the general idea!

PARTY TIME

The best day of the year is my birthday. Oh, yeah . . . it's Miguel's birthday, too. We love it so much that we want to celebrate as much as we can! We also love having an excuse to bring all of our family and friends together!

Miguel and I have gotten so good at celebrating that Mamá and Papi barely even have to do anything. We write up the party lists, think up the theme, and help prepare some of the food and refreshments . . . not to mention decorating the party space! That's the best part! Here are some of our party tips so you can also throw a great fiesta.

Miguel and I often make decorations for our parties. Once, I created streamers out of an old deck of cards that I punched holes in and tied together with string. I also made party hats out of coffee filters that I decorated with everyone's name in glitter. Miguel doesn't like glitter as much as I do, but he did get everyone to make T-shirts of their favorite soccer teams once as party favors! You can borrow these ideas . . . or better yet, come up with your own!

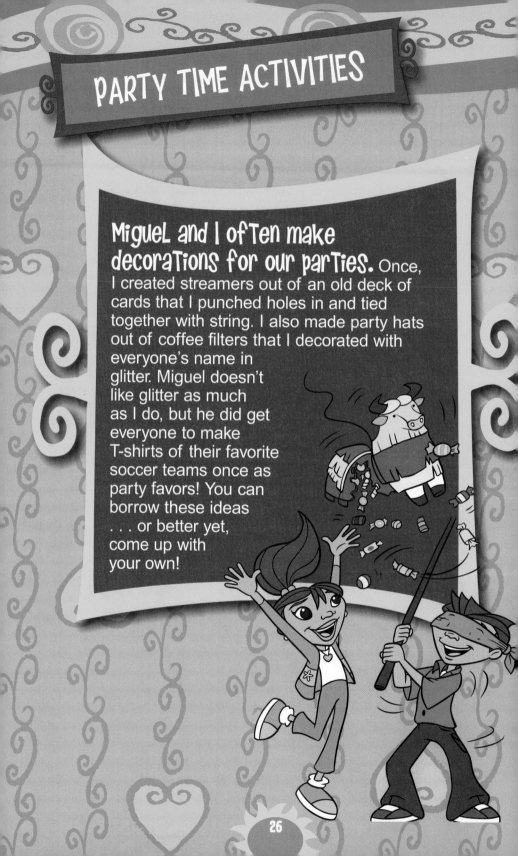

MAKING A PIÑATA

You'll need: glue or paste, old newspapers cut into long strips about 1" thick, a balloon, string, masking tape, paint, and plenty of candy or party favors!

1. Blow up the balloon, tie it, and wrap it with masking tape so you get the shape you want.
2. Dip the newspaper strips into the paste or glue mixture, and stick them onto the balloon. Make sure that it's all covered except for a space where the knotted end of the balloon shows.
3. Repeat the process two more times so that there are three layers of newspaper, and then leave it to dry overnight.
4. Once the piñata has dried, undo the balloon knot or prick the balloon to let the air out.
5. Paint the piñata, add fringe, or cardboard pieces so it resembles a horse, donkey, or anything you like.
6. Put candy or treats into the piñata through the hole where the balloon knot was.
7. Cover the opening with more newspaper strips, and it's ready to hang for your party!

CAREER DAY

SomeTimes I dream abouT whaT I'd Like To be when I grow up. I've always wanted to be a professional soccer player. I think I've got a pretty good kick, but just in case that doesn't work out, I'm always interested in finding out what grown-ups do for a living.

Take Mamá and Papi, for example. They own a pet store. Pretty neat, huh? There are so many things you can do in the world — it's just a matter of picking what you want to do! Try asking grown-ups you know about what they do. Maybe they'll even let you tag along for a day to see what their job is all about.

CAREER DAY ACTIVITIES

CAREER QUESTIONS

⚙ Do you like animals? Maybe you should work with them for a living. You might want to check out becoming a veterinarian, an animal behaviorist, or even a pet-store owner like Maya and Miguel's parents.

⚙ Always writing in your journal, sketching, or doodling? There are lots of jobs in creative fields you can pursue. Try asking a newspaper reporter or graphic design specialist in your community about their jobs.

SETTING UP AN INTERVIEW

When I found out that my classmate's father was an aeronautical engineer, I couldn't wait to ask him some questions. Making rockets sounds so cool! I set up a time to talk to him, and you can do the same!

Make sure you write down questions beforehand, so you'll get all the information you need.

Ask them if you can go to their workplace for a day to see what it's really like.

Ask for them to suggest books or websites you can learn from, too.

WORD SEARCH

Circle the words below in any direction.

Reporter
Doctor
Banker
Teacher
Lawyer

Fireman
Engineer
Psychologist
Designer
Scientist

```
N O P T A R T N M J D K O L
L P S F I R E M A N O Q I T
U I Y I C N A B W C C S E B
J D C D H K K A N R T S K A
P W H E E K K N U E O C J T
W E O R I S K T W P R I E R
S C L K S T I E K O K E I D
M L O A K E R G E R K N R E
I O G K W K O V N T I T A N
S K I T E Y C F K E N I S G
T E S P J O E T A R R S N I
U E T V I S T R R U G T W N
L R T E A C H E R P S M O E
V O U F S S A L C T A P C E
Q U G I N E E R B A N K E R
```

When it rains,

I don't get too sad because . . . guess what? *¡Tengo una idea!* This time, it's a really good idea! Looking through our family's keepsakes is really cool! Miguel and I found some really amazing things in one of Abuela's old trunks: pictures, postcards, and tons of things from when she was a girl!

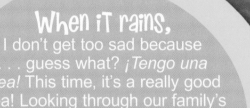

Miguel and I can spend all afternoon looking through Abuela's trunk, and she told us great stories about every object.

Before you go through your family's things, remember to ask your parents or grandparents for permission. Maybe they'll even let you organize old letters and photographs for them!

MAKE A FAMILY TREE!

Start by drawing a diagram of the people you know in your family — you, your sisters or brothers, parents, and grandparents. Write your name at the bottom, and work up from there. Ask relatives to fill in names where you're not sure, and fill in the rest

Robert Santos — Isabel Santos

Ernesto Chavez — Elena Chavez

Felix Santos

Santiago Santos — Rosa Santos

Ernesto Chavez — Theresa Chavez

Maya Santos

Miguel Santos

Alberto "Tit Chavez

Abuela told us stories about all of the photographs of her when she was young, but to help her organize it better, I offered to make a scrapbook for her. That way, everyone can see her history on display!

HERE ARE SOME IDEAS FOR MAKING A SCRAPBOOK:

- Organize pictures and other objects chronologically, by event, or by person.

- Have someone write in their memories of events and include them in the scrapbook.

- Start a family history book, using the scrapbook as a visual reference.

- Frame some of your favorite photographs, letters, or mementos.

RECORDING IT

Besides a scrapbook, there's another way to preserve memories. Next time you talk to a relative, try writing it down, tape recording it, or videotaping it. That way, their memories will be kept alive for generations to come. You can even make it a surprise for other members of the family!

PREPARING FOR A PET

Here in The Santos household, we would be lost without Paco. He comes with us everywhere, and loves to chime in on the conversation — even if it isn't really about him. Just kidding, Paco!

If you're thinking of getting a pet, though, there's a wide variety to choose from. Just make sure that you get the right one for you. You'll be welcoming a permanent member into your family, so you'll want to do all the research before you decide.

PET QUIZ

1. My home is best described as:
   A. A closet-sized space, with not much outdoor space.
   B. It's a decent size.
   C. Pretty big with a backyard.
   D. It's practically a palace!

2. In terms of physical activity, I usually
   A. Don't do much! Sleeping is more my speed.
   B. Walk a lot, but don't sweat.
   C. I'm active, and I love trying new things.
   D. Never slow down!

3. I live:
   A. In an urban area.
   B. Just outside a city.
   C. In the suburbs.
   D. A place where there's lots of nature and wide, open spaces.

If you answered mostly:

As: A small, low-maintenance pet is your best bet. Fish, a lizard, or a bird — any animal that doesn't require a lot of space.

Bs: Try a cat, rabbit, or a lap dog. They don't take as much time as a bigger animal, and don't need as much room.

Cs: A mid-sized dog might fit your active lifestyle.

Ds: Anything goes — if you've got the space, why not take advantage of it? From large dogs to horses, you have the room and lifestyle to take care of almost any pet.

PET-PROOFING YOUR HOME

So you've finally made a decision about what pet to get? Congratulations! Next, to welcome your new friend into your home, you've got to prepare for its arrival. Here's a list to help you:

- Find an area for your pet — a birdcage, aquarium, kitty litter box, or dog bed all need a spot to be placed.

- Inspect the areas where your pet will live, and make sure nothing dangerous is found there, like cleaning materials, small toys, or sharp objects.

CHORE SCHEDULE

Maya and I share the chores of taking care of Paco, but just so you make sure you're taking good care of your new pet, I created a schedule for every day of the week. Maybe this will help you — and let your parents know how responsible you are!

	Monday	Tuesday	Wednesday	Thursday	Friday	Saturday	Sunday
AM Feeding:							
AM Exercise:							
Changing the Water:							
Cleanup:							
PM Feeding:							
PM Exercise:							

CHARITY DRIVE

My favorite ideas are the ones that help out my friends,

family, and neighbors. I love coming up with ideas that benefit the whole community . . . like holding a charity drive!

Check with your local community charities — they probably have organizations you can join. Or if not, try starting one of you own, like a canned food drive, or getting together friends and collecting old clothes to give to charity. It doesn't take much time out of your schedule, and it always feels good to help other people out!

CHARITY DRIVE ACTIVITIES

YOUTH VOLUNTEERING

Get in touch with the volunteer organization in your community, and they can put you in contact with many different organizations. Check with your school, too, for ways you can get more involved. Once you do research, maybe you can even open up a chapter of your favorite organization!

Here's some information on national organizations with programs for kids:

AMERICAN RED CROSS:
http://www.redcross.org/services/youth/0,1082,0_326_,00.htm

HABITAT FOR HUMANITY:
http://www.habitat.org/ccyp/youth.html

YOUTH VOLUNTEER CORPS OF AMERICA:
http://www.yvca.org/yvca/index.cfm

HOLIDAY CHARITY PROJECTS

Don't forget that holidays are an important time to remember people in need! Try starting a Thanksgiving food collection, or a gift drive during Christmas or Easter. It's easy to do! Here are a few tips:

◎ Get an adult to supervise your project.

◎ Pick a church, synagogue, homeless shelter, or another organization that you want to help.

◎ Set a goal for your donations.

◎ Round up your friends, neighbors, and schoolmates to get involved.

◎ Start a chart to track your progress.

ART PROJECTS

Besides my first Love (soccer, of course!),

I really like to draw. I can do it anywhere — on the bus, at home, and in the classroom at recess. Someday, I'm going to have my own comic book series!

You can be an artist, too, and it doesn't have to be just drawing. Knitting, painting, water coloring . . . the list is endless! Anything that gets your creative juices flowing works. The best part is that you can work with any materials you like. From the plain old crayons that you have at home to supplies you can get at the craft store, everyone can be a artist!

MINI-DICTIONARY OF ART TERMS

Abstract: An art movement in which the appearance of an object is changed by the artist, leaving out details or distorting the image

Background: The part of a two-dimensional work of art that seems farther away from the viewer

Batik: A technique of dying cloth or fabric that originated in Indonesia, resulting in a multi-colored or streaked design

Canvas: A cloth-covered frame used for painting

Collage: A composition with different materials glued and layered onto a two-dimensional surface

Cubism: A form of art that shows many views at one time

Dimension: Width, height, or length

Foreground: The part of a two-dimensional artwork that appears closest to the viewer

Impressionism: An art movement in which the artists tried to capture an immediate image at first glimpse

Kente Cloth: A Ghanaian traditional woven cloth with patterns

Mural: Artwork on a wall or ceiling

Origami: The Japanese art form of folding paper into forms and shapes

Perspective: A technique that artists use to portray three-dimensional images in two dimensions

Proportion: The relation of parts to one another to create balance

Sculpture: A three-dimensional work of art

Still Life: A picture of inanimate objects

MAKING A MASK

Did you know masks have been used in lots of different cultures? You can look up some historic ways they've been used, from Native Americans ritual dances to African tribes to Victorian costume balls. Here are some instructions on how to make one:

HERE'S WHAT YOU NEED:

- A large piece of cardboard or poster board
- A pencil
- Scissors
- Glue
- Crayons or colored pencils
- String or elastic
- A hole puncher

HERE'S WHAT TO DO:

1. Draw a circle or oval on the cardboard a little bit larger than the size of your face and cut it out.

2. Draw holes for the eyes, mouth, and nose and cut those out.

3. Decorate the mask with the historical references you looked up.

4. Punch holes on either side, attach the string or elastic, and presto!

HELPING THE ELDERLY

Maya and I are Lucky that Abuela Lives so close by.

It's easy to visit her, and I know she sometimes needs some help with groceries and moving things around. We're happy to help Abuela — even if she is healthy and strong!

We know some of Abuela's friends aren't as lucky to have their grandkids around, so Maya and I help out some other senior citizens that live nearby when we can. Sometimes we just stop by and chat, too. It can get lonely at the top!

HELPING THE ELDERLY ACTIVITIES

SETTING UP AN INTERVIEW

There are lots of things that we can teach our elders, like how to use the Internet, but we sometimes forget what we can learn from them. After all, they've lived many more decades than we have! Take the time to set up an interview with a neighbor, grandparent, or friend and ask them about an important historical event that they lived through. Write it down, tape record, or videotape it. Who knows? You may even have enough to do a class presentation together with them!

HOW TO VOLUNTEER

Here are some ways you can volunteer your time to the elderly:

Check out a local nursing home or hospital. They often have programs for youth volunteers.

Make a commitment. Know you'll probably have to commit some time each week, so clear out your schedule for a couple of hours.

Even the smallest contribution helps. Every little bit makes a difference in someone's life.

SCAVENGER HUNT

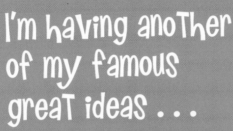

I'm having anoTher of my famous greaT ideas . . .

Why not have a scavenger hunt with all the kids in the neighborhood?

You can hold your own scavenger hunt with your friends and neighbors. Just make sure you have a parent or supervisor with you, or let them know where you are at all times. And make sure you stay within a certain area, too. Or you can even have the hunt take place within your own house!

SCAVENGER HUNT ACTIVITIES

Luckily, you don't need much for a scavenger hunt, only some creative ideas! You can even organize a hunt around a theme, like a historical event, animals, or literature. Here's a few that I came up with that you can borrow, and don't forget to think up some of your own, too! The crazier, the better!

THE ALPHABET HUNT

Find an object that begins with each letter of the alphabet. Hard to find letters like q, x, and z get extra points!

THE NATURE HUNT

Find leaves, berries, or plants. Just make sure everything grows in the area that you'll be searching. And avoid poison ivy!

FOURTH OF JULY HUNT

Find patriotic objects, like something red, white, and blue and other things that mean Independence Day!

WHAT YOU'LL NEED

Luckily most of the things you need for your scavenger hunt are the found objects, but these might help you get started:

- ☼ Paper and pencil to make the list for each group
- ☼ Plastic bags or trash bags for storing your objects
- ☼ A judge
- ☼ Awards for the winners

My friends and family are always calling me super-dramatic, especially Miguel, who often says I was born for the stage! I have an idea that will prove all of them right . . . putting on a play!

Whether you'll be the lead or have the smallest of roles, or even be the director, everyone can get involved. Get a group of friends together to be in your very own stage production. Between writing a script, practicing lines, and finding costumes, there's a lot of work to be done — even if you'll just be performing in the comfort of your own living room.

PLAY TERMINOLOGY

ACT: The division in sections of a play

BACKSTAGE: The area of the stage that the audience can't see

BREAK A LEG: What actors say instead of "good luck"

CAST: The actors in a play

CURTAIN CALL: At the end of a play, when the actors bow

DIALOGUE: The spoken parts or conversations between characters

DOWNSTAGE: Front part of the stage

GREEK THEATER: It originated around 600 B.C., and is the model for plays as we know them today

KABUKI: Japanese theater that uses acting and dancing to tell stories, using heavy makeup for the actors since the female roles are performed by men

MATINEE: The afternoon showing of a play

NOH DRAMA: A type of Japanese theater with elaborate costumes and scenery, and a heroic theme

PANTOMIME: Acting without using spoken words or props

TRAGEDY: A serious drama with a conflict, resolution, and conclusion

UPSTAGE: The back part of the stage

CREATING A STAGE

I usually call all the world my stage, but you can make one for yourself, whether in your own house or backyard:

- Clear an area out for a stage where there's nothing blocking you. If you need to, ask your parents to move furniture for your performance.

- If you can, hang sheets up as temporary curtains, so you'll have a chance to change the set during different acts. Plus, it'll make the performance more exciting.

- Find lightweight tables and chairs that you can use as your props. If you have time, you can even make a few things out of cardboard!

- Make some programs for your audience members.

CUE CARDS

Sometimes we actors forget our lines! But don't worry, there's an easy solution — cue cards! The director, or a helpful friend, holds up a card in the audience with the lines written on it in case emergency strikes! All you'll need is a big poster board and a marker.

YOUR OWN GARDEN

Mmmm — I Love The Smell of Cooking, whether

vegetables are being chopped or the food is right out of the oven! We like using fresh ingredients in my family . . . and what better way to make sure everything's fresh than growing your own? You'll know your herbs or fruits are crisp when you pluck them right off your own plant or tree!

Luckily, plants like avocados are easy to grow. I've learned how do it, and I can show you how to develop your own green thumb. Start by asking a family member to reserve a spot in the window box, fence off a section of the backyard for you, or help you set up a big gardening pot in a sunny location. Pretty soon, you'll be presiding over your very own patch of greenery!

HOW TO START A PLANT

1. Find a ripe avocado pit, or a piece of raw potato.

2. Attach toothpicks to the sides of the pit or potato.

3. Place it in a dish or jar filled with water propped up by the toothpicks so only the 1/3 bottom part of the seed or potato piece touches the water.

4. Place the jar in a sunny spot, and change the water frequently.

5. When you see roots begin to develop, take the plant and placed in potted soil. Soon, you'll have your own household plant.

6. If you have a backyard and live in a sunny climate, you can transfer your plant to the backyard.

A GARDENING JOURNAL

Whatever you decide to grow, keep a gardening journal where you can record and track the growth of your plant every day or every week. Start small with plants like avocados, radishes, or sunflower and pumpkin seeds, before graduating onto other larger and harder-to-grow plants. It will be really amazing to look back once the little seed starts to flower or becomes a tree!

	Growth Progress	Color	Root Length	Other Notes
DAY 1				
DAY 2				
DAY 3				
DAY 4				

CONCLUSION

Super-fabuloso!

We sure hope you had fun with this book.

Don't stop improving your world after completing these activities. Go out and invent your own . . . and make everywhere around you a better place!